FOR GRANDPA BEAR CG AND HIS NAVITATE YEMAYA XOL. — XELENA

FOR YOU WHO OBSERVE SILENTLY AND MOVE MIRACULOUSLY. — ADRIANA

ALL AROUND US

By Xelena González • Illustrated by Adriana M. García

Cinco Puntos Press
www.cincopuntos.com

GRANDPA SAYS CIRCLES ARE ALL AROUND US. WE JUST HAVE TO LOOK FOR THEM.

HE POINTS TO THE RAINBOW THAT RISES HIGH IN THE SKY AFTER A THUNDERCLOUD HAS COME.

"THE REST OF IT IS DOWN BELOW, IN THE EARTH, WHERE WATER AND LIGHT FEED NEW LIFE. THAT'S THE PART WE CANNOT SEE."

GRANDPA AND I WORK SIDE BY SIDE IN THE GARDEN, PLANTING FLOWERS AND PULLING VEGETABLES.

WE EAT WHAT WE'VE GROWN—CRUNCHY LETTUCE, SWEET CARROTS AND SPICY CHILES.

GRANDPA AND I TAKE A WALK AROUND OUR NEIGHBORHOOD.

WE STARE AT THE GREEN AND BROWN RINGS IN EACH OTHER'S EYES FOR A LONG TIME, AND THEN WE LAUGH AGAIN.

"I'LL SHOW YOU ONE MORE IMPORTANT CIRCLE BEFORE THE BIG, ROUND MOON COMES OUT," SAYS GRANDPA.

WE WALK WAY BACK IN OUR YARD AND SIT UNDER A TALL PECAN TREE.

GRANDPA SEEMS SAD WHEN HE SITS HERE, BECAUSE THIS IS WHERE WE BURY THE ASHES OF OUR ANCESTORS. I DON'T REMEMBER THEM, BUT HE DOES.

"EVEN OUR BODIES RETURN TO THE EARTH," HE SAYS AND PATS THE GROUND WITH HIS BIG HANDS.

"BUT THAT'S ONLY HALF OF THE CIRCLE.
THAT'S THE PART WE CANNOT SEE."

FINALLY, WE WALK TO THE FRONT YARD TO
WATER OUR SMALLEST TREE. GRANDPA PLANTED
IT FOR ME ON THE DAY I WAS BORN, AND
EVERYTHING THAT FED ME WHILE I GREW IN
MY MOTHER'S BELLY IS BURIED AT THE ROOTS.
I LOVE BRINGING WATER TO THE APPLE TREE
THAT IS ALREADY TALLER THAN I AM.

DEAR READER,

When I was six, I was given a class assignment to draw a timeline of my life. Birth was the beginning. First steps and first fallen tooth were milestones. I wondered aloud how my timeline would continue, and more importantly, how it would end.

My father shook his head when he heard me. "People will tell you it's a line, but we believe it's a circle," he said, gathering two imaginary points of a timeline and joining them midair to form a circle. By "we," he meant our family of four, as well as our larger family of people, whom we call *mestizos*. This name refers to our biracial mix of Native American and Spanish ancestry.

We were taught to revere our elders, even those who had passed on. We were also taught not to fear death, as it is an essential part of life. In my family, we have cremated our relatives who have passed on, but we do not bury the ashes, as the family does in the story. This is from my imagination—a nice way of returning to the times of ancestral burial grounds and family plots. It is the way I wish to return to the earth.

Like the family in the story, we *do* plant our children's placentas after birth. This is a custom practiced by many cultures around the world, most notably the Navajos of America and the Maori of New Zealand. We find this practice, along with the art of gardening, to be a vital way of re-connecting with the earth, especially our little piece of land where my family has lived for five generations.

These days it seems more people are finding ways of honoring the earth and their ancestors. More people are creating birth and death rituals that are right for their families. And more people are seeing themselves as part of a greater circle.

Thank you for opening this book and opening your mind to the ideas inside.

—XELENA GONZÁLEZ

FIRST EDITION

10 9 8 7 6 5 4 3 2

Library of Congress Cataloging-in-Publication Data

Names: Gonzalez, Xelena, author. | Garcia, Adriana M., illustrator.
Title: All around us / by Xelena Gonzalez ; illustrated by Adriana M. Garcia.
Description: First edition. | El Paso, Texas : Cinco Puntos Press, [2017] |
   Summary: Finding circles everywhere, a grandfather and his granddaughter
   meditate on the cycles of life and nature.
Identifiers: LCCN 2017014877 | ISBN 9781941026762 (hardback)
9781941026786 (e-book)
Subjects: | CYAC: Circle—Fiction. | Nature—Fiction. | Life cycles (Biology)—
Fiction. | Grandfathers—Fiction. | BISAC: JUVENILE FICTION / Family
/ Multigenerational. | JUVENILE FICTION / Social Issues / Friendship.
| JUVENILE FICTION / Social Issues / Death & Dying. | JUVENILE
FICTION / Nature & the Natural World / Environment.
Classification: LCC PZ7.1.G6533 Al 2017 | DDC [E]—dc23
LC record available at https://lccn.loc.gov/2017014877

ADRIANA M. GARCIA is an artist who has worked with acrylic and oil for over 20 years. For *All Around Us*, however, she ventured into the world of digital creation. Using a graphics tablet with a stylus pen and working in a painting software program, she created the illustrations for this book. Adriana took photos of Xelena's father and daughter as references to inspire the illustrations in this, her first picture book.

A NOTE ON THE TYPE: The story for this book is set in the contemporary typeface Lemon Yellow Sun designed by Hanoded. It is tall, with all caps and named after a line from its creator's favorite Pearl Jam song, *Jeremy*. The rest of the type (like this type you are now reading) is set in Adobe Caslon. It is a serif font first designed by William Caslon in 1722. Benjamin Franklin used it extensively and in fact it was the font used to set both the Declaration of Independence and the U.S. Constitution.

Design by Anne M. Giangiulio

APR   2018